Who is Jes

By Olivia Bryan Updegrove

Illustrated by Nicole Lapointe

DEDICATION

To my children, Tyke and Annajane.
May you always know the depths and joys of faith!

"Who is Jesus?" she asked as she was tucked into bed.

"He died on a cross and then rose from the dead.

He is the Son of God who came to this Earth.

He taught us of life, death, and rebirth."

"So?" said the child who did not understand.
"What's all the fuss about this Jesus Christ man?"

"You'll learn as you grow. Now go to bed!"

"No!" said the child and she pulled up her head.

The woman sat down on
the bed by the child.
"I guess this is going to
take quite a while."

The child calmed her face and drew
close her bear.
The woman spoke slowly to her
curious ears.

"There is no way to tell you this all in one night,
   but pay close attention, I'll tell the highlight.

From Christmas church lessons you may recall
   that Jesus was born to be King of us all.
So after he was born in the manger one night
   it seems Mary and Joseph raised him alright.

"We then do not know about Jesus the child.
How he played, what he liked or if he was wild."

The girl giggled as she thought of Jesus the boy.
She wondered if he had any really cool toys.

DIVINE: Really, really, really, really special in a BIG God way.

"It means more special than we humans here."

"So let me make sure I am getting this clear. Jesus was more special than we humans here?"

"It depends on what you grow up to believe.
'Cause everyone's special in God's great story."

"But," said the woman, "There was something different.
His story shows lots of BIG God commitment."

"Wait! Before we go on to what happens next.
I want to make sure I get all of this.

So after he was born in the manger one night
it seems Mary and Joseph raised him alright.
Then at age 12, Jesus did show some signs
that he was preparing to be God's Divine."

"Next, he was baptized and gathered
      his friends
(Twelve disciples, along with both
      women and men).
With Jesus as their leader this group
      traveled 'round.
Healing sick, changing lives,
      they went town to town.

At times he'd share parables, or stories, with the people.
His miracles of faith were SO unbelievable."

"A parable," the child thought out loud to her bear.
She looked in his eyes and continued to share.

"Jesus was baptized and gathered his friends,
      (Twelve disciples, along with both women and men).
With Jesus as their leader this group traveled 'round.
      Healing sick, changing lives, they went town to town.
At times he'd share parables, or stories, with the people.
      His miracles of faith were SO unbelievable."

"There were so many wonderful things that he did!
Make sure you keep asking when you're not just a kid.

You know that his story still matters today,
He taught us to live in more sacred ways.
He taught us to love even those who are mean,
He taught us to help those folks in great need.

The 'Body of Christ,' we are all a big part,
   Love brings us together and strengthens God's heart.
But when people split by age, race, and more,
   We weaken the love that Jesus worked toward."

"Wow!" That's a lot of ideas in my brain.
"Give me a moment so I can explain.

I know that his story still matters today,
He taught us to live in more sacred ways.
He taught us to love even those who are mean,
He taught us to help those folks in great need.

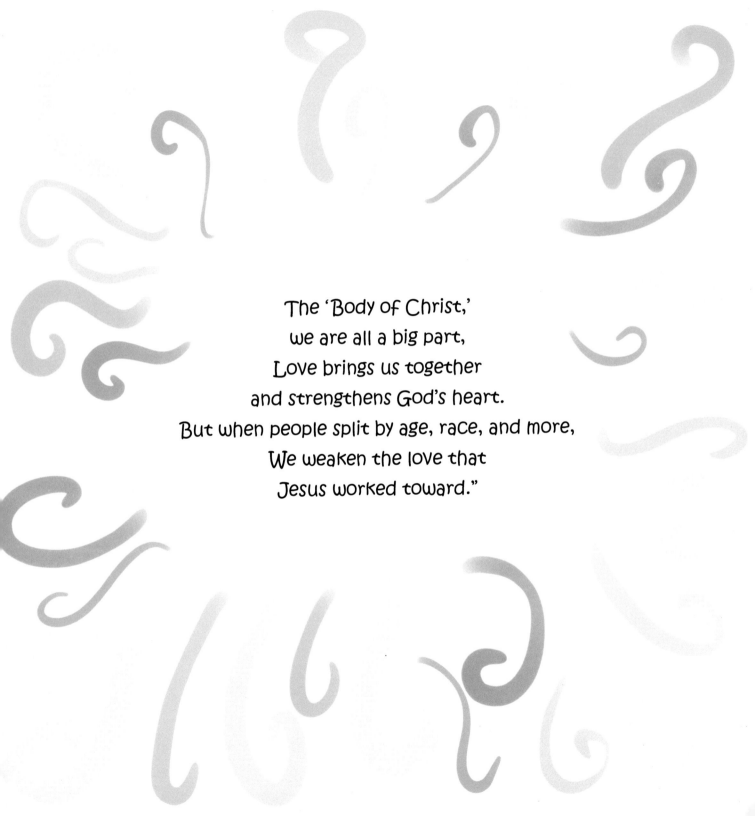

The 'Body of Christ,'
we are all a big part,
Love brings us together
and strengthens God's heart.
But when people split by age, race, and more,
We weaken the love that
Jesus worked toward."

Then both of them knew as they sat on the bed
the part of the story that fills Christians with dread.

They looked at each other. They both knew this part.
The part that with tears breaks each of our hearts.

"Jesus then died on the cross," whispered the girl.
"There was no other way to help show the world."

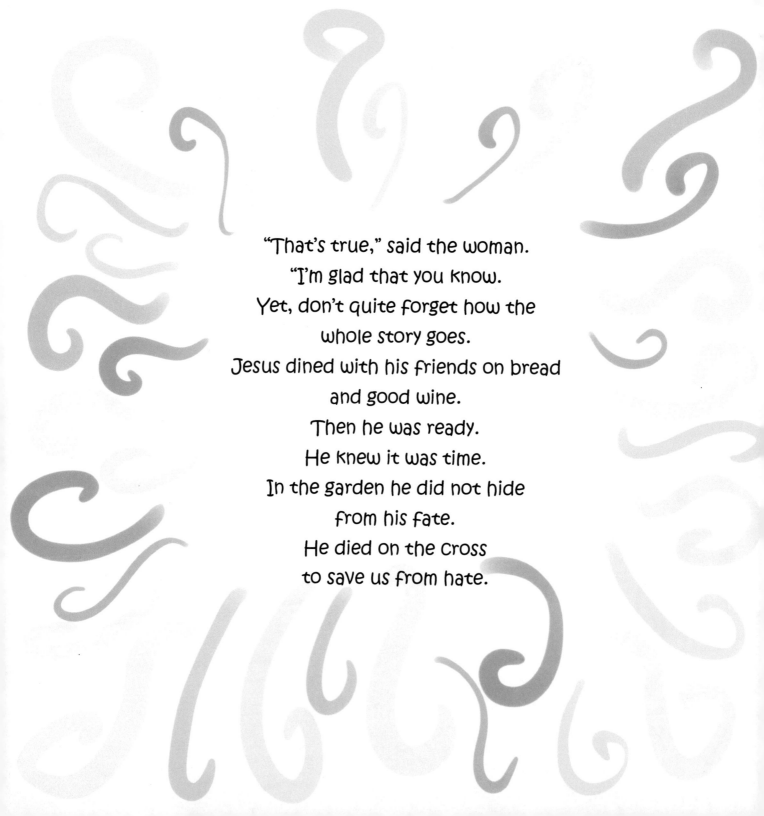

"That's true," said the woman.
"I'm glad that you know.
Yet, don't quite forget how the
whole story goes.
Jesus dined with his friends on bread
and good wine.
Then he was ready.
He knew it was time.
In the garden he did not hide
from his fate.
He died on the cross
to save us from hate.

But then three days later friends saw him alive!
So we know that a life lived with God will survive!

And God's still with Jesus, and both are with you...
Watching and loving... 'cause that's what they do."

"That's what they do," the child yawned and said.
Slowly her head fell back on her bed.

The woman laid the bear by the small sleeping girl.
Then she silently thanked Jesus for helping the world.

About the Author

Rev. Dr. Olivia Bryan Updegrove serves as a minister for Families & Children on multiple national and local levels with the Christian Church, Disciples of Christ. She also serves as a mother, wife, daughter, sister, and aunt to a wonderful family.

About the Illustrator

Although Nicole was born in Detroit, she was raised in the peace and tranquility of the northern woods on a lake. With nary another child within miles, she spent most of her childhood drawing, talking to squirrels, and pretending to be a Jedi. Bored, Nicole moved many times and finally returned as a full-fledged adult (lol) to her roots in Detroit. She still talks to squirrels, thinks she's a Jedi, and continues to draw relentlessly.

Made in the USA
Middletown, DE
21 September 2016